I0539187

Tales from Hearts

Compiled & Edited By
Sourav Chatterjee and Priyanka Saraf

INKQUILLS®
FOR THE READERS, BY THE WRITERS

Published by InkQuills Publishing House
www.inkquills.in

First Edition 2019
All Rights Reserved. Copyright © 2019

ISBN: 978-81-934088-9-6

DEDICATION

Late Grandmother Karuna Mukherjee;
You will stay in our heart forever…
                                    -- Sourav Chatterjee

Dedicated to all those people who fail to express
what they feel…
                                    -- Priyanka Saraf

ACKNOWLEDGEMENT BY SOURAV

I would like to show my gratitude to all the wonderful people in my life.

First of all, I would like to say thanks to my Best friend, Sayan Chakrabarty, for your support in every phases of my life. Thanks for your support and inspiration! You made me realize the meaning of Friendship! Thanks for understanding me more than anyone, thanks for accepting my real self and motivating me towards the journey of Writing!

Thanks to my Parents for your moral support and your blessings in every step of my life!

Thanks to my elder brother Chayan Chatterjee for your support and helping me in every step of life!

Special thanks to my lovely cousins Mamai, Piu for lovely company, my friend of crime! I just can't describe how much I love you in words...!!

Thanks my loving sister Atasi for all those Craziness, thanks for making me smile!

Thanks to my best friend Ponam... Sorry, Pro... oops, sorry again... Prodipta, for your craziness and hanging out with me when no one else was there for me! Thanks for listening my every story and tolerating my angry and mad side! Thanks for those memorable scooty rides! Enough! I can't praise more!

My school friends- Shayamsundar, Tanusree, Debarpita, Tamogno, Shubhomoy, Sanjib,thanks for the all beautiful memories!

My best buddies Sandip, Suraj, Subhajit for all the bike rides! And for being with me always!

My friend Sanchaita(Mimi), for making me realize that it doesn't matter how long you know each-other but it's about how to understand someone from the very first day when you meet them.

My College friends Abhijit, Manashrita, Silvia, Ritika for your support and memories!

And thanks to my all online friends for being too good and helping and guiding me for my writing!

Thanks Doctor Nadine Brune for saving my life many times! Thanks for being so humble and supportive!

A special thanks to my Co-Editor, Priyanka Saraf for believing me, and for being so humble.

Thanks to whole team of InkQuills for making my dream into reality!

ACKNOWLEDGEMENT BY PRIYANKA

Thanks to my grandpa and parents whose moral support and encouragement made it possible for me to accomplish my dreams.

And, to all the friends who shared their support, without whom I wouldn't have made it this far, thank you.

I extend my sincere thanks to Mr. Sourav Chatterjee, for his sincere guidance, who made it possible to publish this book.

Thanks to all the participants for their patience and coordination.

And a special thanks to the whole team of InkQuills Publishing House.

Above all, to Lord Ganesha, for his countless blessings.

SOURAV CHATTERJEE

Sourav is an avid reader, writer, actor, nature lover. He is also passionate about photography and film direction.

He born and brought up in Asansol, West Bengal.

He worked in the project of "Future of the Past" (Preservation of Heritage) in Kolkata.

He worked internationally as a Communicator and Story teller.

His writings have been published in different books.

He is always eager to learn new things, meet new people and explore new places.

He did his schooling from Dhadka N.C.L. Vidyamandir, Asansol and was the topper from Arts dept. He is also a diploma holder in Communication from Burdwan University. After that he completed his bachelor's degree in Media Science (Hons).

Currently working in films and as a full time Writer.

Email: Sourav.chatterjee8759@gmail.com

Instagram: @souravchatterjee8293

An Open Letter To My Love
(SOURAV CHATTERJEE)

Dear Love,

Have you ever realized how much you broke me down…!?

I'm just waiting for you for so long, but you never came, you even haven't called me for once by yourself! I tried to tell you so many times but, you know I become speechless whenever I'm with you… I just can't describe what actually happening with me right now! You broke me down… You made me cry badly… Yup, after a long time I cried! My tears are just now dry. You know still, right now I'm just scrolling my phone gallery, its full of your picture only, those pictures with you, those beautiful memories I will never forget… But right now, when I'm watching those photos of ours, are just making me cry…!! The pain is really unbearable!! Intolerable!!

I know it will be very hard, maybe impossible for me, but I will try… I will try to forget you, I know I can't and it will break my heart more badly but you know, I totally lost myself in the process of chasing you … Believe me, I can't hate you, never!!

I will love you forever like the same way I did before. But now my silent love will be numb…!!

Yours
Forever

PRIYANKA SARAF

 Priyanka Saraf is an ENTC engineer and currently working as Director in a startup.

She lives in Pune, Maharashtra. She loves to pen down her thoughts through poetry.

Recently she published her debut poetry book *'Rainbow of Thoughts'*. Also, her work has been previously published in various anthologies. Also, she likes to study Indian culture. She is interested in English literature and Indian mythology.

She wants to write about social issues. She believes that there is something good in everyone. Working for the betterment of the society is the main motive in her life.

She is thankful to her family and friends for all the success in her life.

You can get in touch with her through
Email: *priyankasaraf021@gmail.com*
Instagram: *@priyankasaraf021*
Wordpress: *sarafpriyanka.wordpress.com*

Open letter To The Sun
(PRIYANKA SARAF)

Dear Sun,

Please rise early today. I am tired of the undying darkness. I have lost my faith in goodness. Will the things change again? Can I trust everything around me again? I have become doubtful.

Today evening, when you were setting, there was a fear that was worrying me; the fear that you won't rise again. I was losing my hope that the things won't get better again. I was afraid of losing everything again. And now, as it's already dark, all my happiness is broken. I am feeling like I am dead already!

The only hope I am living for is that you would gift me a new life; a life with new hope. A hope to live again; a hope to rise again. I want to see life in the world again. I can't wait to get back to all the special things meant only for me.

So, please Sun can you wake up early today?

Yours

Forever admirer

CONTRIBUTING WRITERS

Abhilash Bijwe

He is a mechanical engineer, entrepreneur. Passion for writing make him write the poems, shayris and short stories.

He is a learner of theosophy, which is study of philosophy science and religion, he is a member of theosophical society Pune lodge.

He believes that words have magic, can make a difference in life. He is always trying to simplify the life of people. That can make the value creation in society.

Abhilash Bijwe

MY LIFE

It's time to make a peace with mind
War between mind and heart goes wild
I want to lose my all to become free from everything
Nothing matter for me more than the destiny

So many smiling outside suffering inside
Better to die in once than take slow poison everyday
Standing in crowd, waiting for perfect moment to find
But it ain't coming, I need to do something

I can't leave it up to the FATE
I want to make my own street
This path is lonely but here joy obviously
Answers are unfolding words are misleading
Universe help me to get out of this shot slowly

I just need to get ready
To fight the demon inside me
Cause it's a pain and suffering
We all have to face alone along the swing

Excuses are like suicide ,It makes life living hell
I stop being what they told me
I becoming I be enjoying myself lonely.

Abhipsa Mohanty

Abhipsa is an English literature student, currently in the IIIrd year of Graduation.

Having been always passionate about writing, she has been penning down her thoughts for different websites and magazines.

An advocate of feminism and realism, she wishes to motivate people and help make a change.

She had been chosen among the best hundred writers of across seven South-Asian nations in 2014, after which she seeks to venture into the life of a successful author. In her works, she likes to explore the different patterns of the human psyche.

Apart from writing, reading and painting also interest her.

Abhipsa Mohanty

THE MIST

The snow falls heavily;
Hidden are the sun, the skeleton trees;
No souls in sight anywhere;
A storm is on the threshold of this scanty town.
Peace is meager,
For the cold, soggy atmosphere
Is uncomfortable.

Food is little, and no hot drinks;
Communication and firewood are all burnt away;
Stranded I am in my poor old man's cabin;
Every morning thin, wispy fingers of the cold mist
Grip the heart.
This tiredness and impatience
Is intolerable.

The gods won't have mercy;
And no one will bother;
The blanket is rugged,
And the rusty heater shall soon give up.
The cold mist grips tighter and tighter every day,
Death will freeze my body anytime,
With no one to cry upon it.
But the thing that cheers me in dearth
Is that I shall probably meet the eternity
On the same day
When Father Christmas celebrates Jesus' birth.

SUNDOWN

As the sun hides behind the trees,
I have nowhere to hide my face;
At each sundown, down sink my spirits…
With the crunch of the yellow leaves
Under my heavy tread, I hear
The crunches of my breaking heart.
But the tears refuse to emerge,
They are all spent.
Ashen, I trudge along the lonely aisle
Into my lonely world,
Too weak and tired to complain.
A breeze rustles the nerves,
A memory of the distant past stirs;
I open the doors of my old house
And the recollections make a ghoulish visit.
Each object I see, possess,
Is an agonizing mockery
For the promises made to be forgotten.
The assurance of a tender touch, a soft kiss
Are for some other handsome woman now.
Miserable is how I continue to live;
Hard as I try, I cannot forget
Or forgive.

OPEN LETTER TO PARENTS

Dear Parents,

I'm glad that you didn't kill me straightaway like many people do nowadays. You raised me and even educated me well. Now I'm married in a well-to-do family that you chose for me. Everything is going fine, but I still have a few complaints.

First of all, why didn't you warn me that once I'm married, you were absolutely free to wash your hands off all my responsibilities? And I could no longer seek refuge on your shoulders when my husband and I quarreled about his habits of drinking. Then, what about telling me that one day I would be forced to terminate my career, something that you encouraged me to build from the time I was two? You said that it would look wrong if I married someone of my choice, whom I'd known for years; but you never told me that I'd have to endure sleeping with a stranger every night. And finally, why didn't you tell me that I'd have to forget myself completely and only slave for others once I was married?

I don't know if you have the answers with you. But in case you have the guts, publish your answers somewhere so that many in my situation would benefit.

Yours faithfully,

The Daughter.

Adity Sinha

Adity is a Software Engineer by profession, but her passion for writing is even more profound and intense.

She believes that writing is an exploration where we learn as we go further and beyond the world within our heads.

She started writing at an early age, and with the passage of time, she fell in love with the idea of voicing the human emotions. Writing makes her feel happy and contented at the same time. She is currently working in a software company located at Bangalore.

Gmail: adity.it@gmail.com

Adity Sinha

THE RENDEZVOUS

In the alley of ruptured hopes,
a ray of sunshine is all I look for.
The alley that leads me astray to
nowhere, but to the rendezvous
with poignant melancholy.

I am more like a deserted sky
keeping a tryst with the misty clouds
scudding across the moon.

I just want someone to meet me in
the middle of tomorrow and forever,
where we both walk down the
boulevard with labyrinth of fingers,
and blaze the faded longings
in pertinent of love where heart
still lingers.

Akshay Korde

Akshay korde is an engineer. He lives in Jejuri, Pune.

He loves to write poems and articles. He also loves trekking to forts and making historical models of temples and historical places in India.

He loves to see others smiling. He believes in humanity.

You can contact him through:
akshaykor27@gmail.com

Akshay Korde

FOREVER YOU

Be the beauty that my eyes chase
Be the love that my soul has accepted
Be the unknown path crossed by holding our hands together
Be the smile on my face when I am upset
Be my first hug to forget the whole world
Be the heaven where your lips touch mine
In the game of ups and downs of life, just be mine forever.

Alice Tinna

Alice Tinna is an Engineer by profession.

She cherishes every person in her life and feel that everyone has a purpose to stay in her life.

She loathes to talk about herself a lot, but can be persuaded to do for work and time to time.

You can find her on Instagram with @_hazel_eyed_girl

And you can contact her through: alicetinna@gmail.com

Alice Tinna

LOST

And I lost what I thought was mine,
I lost the dreams I had in my eyes,
I lost the shine and sparkle of my smile,
I lost the one I considered mine,
I lost the person who didn't told me if he had
anything from his side,
I lost the friend whom I had crossed all the lines,
I lost the hope of sharing same home,
I lost what I had in me since I met him few days ago,
I lost everything tonight,
Now I'm left with empty hands
And ruined smile.

Amit Karavande

Amit Sambhaji Karvandes an engineer.

He lives in Pune.

He loves to write Marathi poems, short stories & Quotes.

He also like write on social issues. Working for the betterment of society is the main motive of his life.

You can get in touch with him

Email: akaravande@gmail.com

OPEN LETRER TO THE MOVIE 'JAB WE MET'

Thank you for teaching me that life is a platform & love is a train. Missing one train is not that bad... The train that is meant for you will lead you towards your perfect destination.

******

To the character 'Aditya'

Dear Aditya,

Thank you for explaining me the real meaning of LOVE.

Thank you for making me believe that love is not a crime & life is not a court room. Thank you for teaching me that if you can love a person at his worst times, you definitely deserve him at his best. You taught me that if someone has left you that wasn't your fault at all. It's also the other person's loss. You made me realize that to become someone like Geet is not much easy. It needs a lot of courage & and also a pure heart. To become Geet, all you need is selfless love. Thank you for teaching me that, to be someone like Geet is a pride and not shame.

Thank you, for making me SMILE again.

******

To the character 'Anshuman'

Dear Anshuman

Thank you for showing me the other side of life. Thank you for making me realize that each girl like Geet should meet someone like Anshuman, who teaches her a lesson to make her realize what she shouldn't do in her life. Thank you for teaching me that you can't force anyone to fall in love with you. That's because of you, I realized that not every ordinary person can afford my dreams. There's a hidden kid inside me. Love is life, not a deal.

******

To the character 'Geet'

Dear Geet

Thank you so much for making me believe that one can survive alone also. No Anshuman can take your life away. No matter what others think, you should always be your own favorite.

You taught me that people like you and me exist in this world & that if you wanna hold on people like Anshuman, make sure that you are ready to experience how hell really feels like.

You taught me that love isn't bad or good. It only decides whom you're going to meet in your life.

And, at last, thank you for making me realize that my smile will light up the world of all the people around me. And, no matter wherever I may reach one day, I am sure that I'll find my true love.

- A Fan of 'Jab We Met'

Anshika

Anshika hails from the city of nawabs; i.e. Lucknow, Uttar Pradesh.

She has completed her graduation in Bachelor of Commerce.

Currently she is preparing for government jobs.

Her hobbies are basically singing and writing. Also she loves to inspire people. Though she is not a professional writer but she has a confidence in herself that readers will be satisfied with her work and they will relate to it.

Her love for writing is not from childhood.
Writing happened to her in the year 2016 after her heartbreak. And now she is proud of it that it happened to her.

She has written for few of the anthologies, they are about to come in mere future.

Email: anshynishad1994@gmail.com
Insta Id: @shayraanshy_

THE VILLAIN SIDE

Every person has 2 sides of himself
One he shows to everyone
Which is very sweet also...
& the other one which he
Doesn't shows to anyone.
For example - * The Villain * side.

In short,
I just wanted to say that everyone
Has a Villain within themselves.
No matter how much you deny
But it's true.

A Villain s side of a person is not
Completely good nor bad...
But, it's just a emotion which comes
Out randomly or when sum1 is in
Anger.

Antara Guha

Antara Guha is a poet by passion since 2015 and published with different publishers.

She is also associated with Poetic Events held across India.

Being a mother of 5 years old she loves spending time with her daughter when she is not writing.

A BOW DOWN TO HER

If she has not been there ,
What would I be?
What would I be?
I had nothing .
And I was none .
I crossed a long path though .
I lived and breathed too.

If she has not been there,
What would I be?
What would I be?
She has been strong.
She held on to me since long.
I was rigid.
I was rude.
She was patient.
She was soothing my soul.
As a broken Chime
My heart was screaming out.
She got busy, too busy
To stick all my pieces back.
I threw her away.
Got back to her every time.

If she has not been there ,
What would I be ?
What would I be ?
No words to praise her

Nor I know the way to bow down to her.

Antara Guha

If she has not been there ,
What would I be ?
I just had my name.
She taught me " How to be me" !

Anu Lal

Anu Lal is one of India's leading short story writers.

He has written five books of short stories.

His stories, poems, and articles are also published by various national and international journals.

He lives in Kerala, with his family. His wife Dhanya is also a writer and poet.

His latest book is *As I Lay Waiting: A Revenge Story*.

He blogs at *The Indian Commentator*.

NANO TALES

I
Diwali

For her newest status update on Diwali, Minakshi couldn't find an appropriate theme. So she went back to the old-age home to take a selfie with her old mother.

II
Love

"You are a changed man," the wife said.
"No, I am the same," he replied.
"You lied to me those days."
"Never...How?"
"You said you could die for me."

III
Miracle

A soothing expression washed over his face. He had a white dhoti covering his knees. He stooped and took some salt in his cupped hands. And the Empire fell.

Anusree Basu

Anusree Basu is a dental student and the contributing author of five anthologies.

She has worked as a content writer for various websites and has garnered prizes for various writing competitions.

Apart from writing she takes great interest in reading, teaching, cooking and orating. She even scripted and directed a short film.

Few years down the line she sees herself as doctor by the day and writer by the night.

AN OPEN LETTER TO HOUSEWIVES

You must be lost doing some daily chores but I would be glad if you take some time out and read this letter.

I know you chose to make food for your husband than doing data entry for your boss. I know your engineering degree went down the drain but that doesn't mean you don't deserve the respect like the other working women. Just because you don't sit in a cubicle and work, it doesn't devalue your efforts.

Every day you wake up before everyone and cook for the family, you are always the last one to retire to bed. You are the one who makes the house feel like home. Unlike the "working women" you don't have holidays. You are on duty 24*7 for 365 days. You don't work for bonuses but for everyone's happiness.

Next time if anyone belittles you, ignore them and have faith on yourself. As Yard said, "Being a mother and a housewife is a worthy choice for any woman, provided that it's her choice." To all the housewives out there, I salute you for your impeccable hard work and dedication. Walk tall. We are all proud of you.

Your lovingly

Anusree

Ayen Gomez

Ayen Gomez is a proud Filipina.

She came from the City of Love, not Paris in France but Iloilo City Philippines,

She's neither a poet nor a writer.

She's just a lost soul that found comfort in writing.

She writes what she can't say.

For her writing is another way of breathing.

Ayen Gomez

LAUNDRY ROOM

Should I tell you to stop?
When I love things which is rough?
Or I'll turn off the machine and
Centralize my brain on the
Sensation your tongue's givin'
That makin' my eyes spin,

Who says there's a right place
To feel this ultimate kind of bliss
When your naughty fingers
Are fashioning my body to groove,

This should be a laundry day
But my man ,
It's seems you've change
The plan!
When you start to wash your
Tongue on the streambed
Between my thighs,
And in ecstasy we're now both high.

Bhanu Prashanth

Bhanu is an educator, researcher, aspiring author and a child rights activist.

She has a great passion for teaching and writing. She is a voracious reader.

Her writing interest covers fiction, non-fiction, poetry and open letters.

She has also contributed for several anthologies.

She is currently working on two books that will have multiple short stories. She has been working with several NGO's and believes in providing self-less service to society.

She dreams of having her books in her library. A rainy day with her favorite book, in her balcony, sipping coffee.

AN OPEN LETTER TO SELF

Dear me,

I recently read a quote: Be who you were created to be, and you will set the world on fire. Isn't it wonderful? You have been celebrating life since many years. You were humiliated, wounded, stabbed and considered as "good-for-nothing".

You proved wrong. You have proved everything and everyone wrong. You have proved your parents wrong. You have shown them that you can be without them. You have proved you love wrong. You are a person of self-respect and esteem and will not let it go at any cost. Where do you get this spirit from? Where are those scars that has wounded you so much? The scars that you wear with pride now. The head that once was hung down with shame, is held high now. You are doing great. Be the same.

Let your mind be as liberated as ever. As spirited as ever. Hold your head high. Your heart will be wounded again, stabbed again. You bounce back. Show everyone that you are not for granted. Show everyone that you deserve to be happy. Show everyone that you are born to win. Good Luck!

Always amazed by your spirit,

Bhanu

Gautam Mayekar

 Gautam is a white hat hacker (A good boy) who occasionally loves to write.

He is an upcoming author of India's most awaited Hacked Trilogy (First book slated to release by end of this year).

Apart from being a sporadic blogger, he is very much active on all social media platforms.

https://www.facebook.com/gsm.gautam

https://www.yourquote.in/gsm_gautam

http://gautammayekar.blogspot.com/

https://www.instagram.com/gautam.mayekar13

Included in the "Tales From Heart" are his 9 letters which he wrote for "Woh Office Waali Ladki", with no real intent to impress her during the Navaratri Festival.

9 LETTERS

Has anyone ever got smitten by someone so much, that they end up writing 9 letters on 9 colors of Navaratri for her? (And her colorful outfits).

Well, I just did. This Navaratri, I insta-storied her and I am hoping that she applies the colors to these letters and my life.

Letter to that girl in Blue:

So it all began that day, the day I first saw you.

And you were wearing blue.

Have you heard that theory? That when God created the universe; some atoms were placed near each other, and now those atoms always keep levitating towards each other.

Believe it or not, we are those atoms.

Today, as I see you in blue, my heart screams out to you. Alas! The words don't come out of my mouth.

So, all I do is pen down those thought on a white page and make a paper plane of it, which I release out of my window.

I am going to do that on all the Navaratri days with a hope that somehow, it finds you….Out of the blue ☺

Letter to that girl in Yellow:

I looked at you in Yellow and wondered. I may not have had my "yellow umbrella" moment yet.

But when your piercing gaze shredded my heart into tiny pieces, it was your yellow top that mended it back into one blood pumping piece.

Yellow is the color of optimism, hope and happiness after all.

Will you be my yellow forever? ☺

Letter to that girl in Green:

I looked at you in green and wondered, there was too much greenery around but why your green was so different?

Our eyes didn't meet, yet your sheer presence around me had my heart skipping its beats. It was the vibrance of your green color top that calmed it down, embracing it and slowly singing a lullaby.

Green signifies energy; nature and surroundings filled with harmony.

FYI, it also signifies greed.

Allow me to be a little "greeny" and ask you-

Will you be my surrounding forever? ☺

Letter to that Girl in Gray:

I looked at you in Gray and wondered, why on a day which is dedicated to Devi Chandraghata (one who carries half-moon over her forehead), your cute full moon like face brightening my heart so much?

It is only when I looked at your gray top, that my heart came out of its flashing yet translucent state to normalcy.

Gray is the color of practicality, maturity, responsibility as well as boredom.

I am a bit gray. In this flashy world full of unrealistic expectations, will you be my practical forever? ☺

Letter to that girl in Orange:

I looked at you in........wait! Hold on. Does it even matter anymore?

I have started seeing you just about anywhere and everywhere now.

The color Orange symbolizes warmth, happiness and energy. Something which I have found lately with your serendipitous arrival.

Today is the day of Goddess Kushmanda, they say she is so powerful, that she lives in the sun.

Will you be my orange and stay in my heart forever? ☺

Letter to that girl in White:

I looked at you in white.... Actually no, I couldn't make the eye contact, damn!

And yet, while your exquisite smile in orange took my sleep and breath away, your white top brought the life back.

White not only signifies peace and purity, it also means perfection and New beginnings.

Somewhere between these colors of Navaratri, I have stumbled upon the perfection which is you. And I have this feeling in the tiny corner of my heart that you could be "the one", the beginning of something new, us.

Gets on his knees

Let's be each other's white forever? ☺

P.S. Dying to see you in red.

Letter to that girl in Red:

I looked at you in red and didn't just wonder, I died for a few seconds. Consider it as a mini heart attack. While in heaven, I wrote a tiny poem, but it's too cheesy and lame to upload here. so, chuck it.

The color red symbolizes passion, adventure and seduction; something which your fiery eyes possess. And it is the reason why my mind is being little naughty and imaginative.

Yet, I will hold those thoughts back and say what I genuinely feel about you.

I say, that your bold and glam avatar appeals to the wicked sarcastic Virgo in me and we are definitely going to have fun ☺ but it is your aura as whole that passes the front porch test somehow.

There is a magnetic pull in you which I can't withstand anymore, I am getting closer and closer, like a child excited about his ice cream or a gift.

Would you like to be this child's permanent gift of forever in a red wrapping paper? ☺

Letter to that girl in Sky Blue:

I don't even know, if you know that I am writing this to you and whether you wait for these letters as much as I wait for your "view". But I got asked by 10-12 people today "when is the next letter coming?", so "yay!" ☺

There is a TV series I grew up watching where in the starting scene the main character Ted looks at the girl near the counter and says, "someday I am gonna marry her"

I had that exact same feeling about you in the same situation and that's the biggest compliment I can give you.

It is not your beauty that sets you apart, there are some strange soulful waves, an unexplainable longing which makes me stutter whenever you are around, like how peacocks sense the arrival of rains.

Sky blue is for faith, heaven, trust. Universe will show some signs today, if it really believes in me and my words, it will rain tonight.

Under the guidance of universe, I wish to build a heaven with you.

Will you be my faith forever?

Tales from Hearts

Letter to that girl in Pink:

Missed me? I think you did.

Perhaps that's the reason why it rained so much. I am telling you, universe is shedding quite a bit of happy tears as we are connecting somewhere in some parallel universe. And that day isn't far when we connect here on the earth. Cupids have started working; a bright white love pigeon came and sat in my balcony today. I am sure you sent it, didn't you? Don't lie.

Pink is the color of tenderness; sweet, nice, playful romance. Something which I promise you till the eternity. Pink also represents the innocence of child which resides in all of us. Yes, the same child who wants you wrapped up in red as his gift, the same child whose eyes lit up in all the colors of you that he saw.

They say, it is also the universal color of love.

As discussed already, the universe is with us ☺

It's only you who has to answer now. Will you accept my love and paint it in pink, forever? ☺

Letter to that girl in All Colors:

So this is it? Our tryst with nine colors end here?

Don't you feel this inexplicable void? An emptiness.

Why did I ask the universe for rains? I should have asked for infinite colors instead; that this festival never ends (infinite-ratri maybe)

From magnetic pull to universal phenomenon, you have swept me off. What started just as a way of complementing you, quickly became an emotional ride for me. The process of writing began easy. But now, the heaviness of my heart makes it all the more difficult to finish it.

Let's just say that all your colors have formed a rainbow for me knocking over my heart's closed door. And just as rainbow symbolizes transformation of life, I am hoping you be that new found life for me.

Be my rainbow. Give me some signs will you? say something, Anything. Find me and I will find you.

Let these letters be legendary and our story become the one which we tell our grandkids about...

Will you be my forever, forever? ☺

.

Geetanjali Kapoor

As the name suggest, Geetanjali is a "collection of poems" for her family.

She loves to write; she is soft hearted beautiful person who has nothing to do with this harsh world.

She just wants to bring good enough through her words so that humanity will exist ever and forever.

Geetanjali Kapoor

SO, SHE NEVER DEPART

She is like a baby bird, who always wants to fly,
like an illusion of water in a deep dreary sigh.
A Barbie doll whose beauty never frowns,
A giggle on a serious dark face.
The kindest and devil as well,
A complete set in itself.

Mind it, she is not a history whom you ever want to
create,
Nor a mystery whom you can crack.
She illuminates your life and dazzle you in every gaze,
Undoubtedly, a creator and a destroyer in itself.
She, is a complete package of all relation with a
perfect set of emotion.

So, if so much to have, what is the reason to collapse.
Come, "Let us do our part, so she never depart."

Gurpreet Arora

Gurpreet Arora is a Freelance writer and lives in New Delhi.

She has a degree in B.A programme from Delhi University.

She writes poem basically.

In her free time, she loves to play badminton.

Reading is just not a hobby for her but a passion which inspires her to write.

She is a funjabi girl loves to enjoy every moment of life.

Gurpreet Arora

I REMEMBER

I Remember that day when I saw u in the dark light;
When the stars twinkle at night.
I Remember that day when I cry sometimes;
and u wipe my tears all night.
I Remember that day when u wore my gifted shirt,
and u take me home by long drive.
I Remember that day when we talk all night and the
morning on their bright.
I Remember that day, that morning, that evening, that
night.
I Remember all those moments which i could enjoy
with you.
Now the days has been passed u aren't here for
holding my hands.
I cherish those moments which could never be aside...

Jangili Naresh Kumar

Jangili Naresh Kumar resides in Hyderabad and a well-known hotelier.

After completion of Bachelor's degree in Science, he chosen to enter into hotel management and presently enjoying his Profession as a chef with an excellent command in making European and Indian food.

His hobbies are writing, reading fictions and love to prepare tasty food in his kitchen.

He can be contacted on j.naresh2498@gmail.com

Instagram:-   @chef_n_salt
              @color_blinds

SOULMATES

Days gone...
Years gone...
Centuries gone...
Births gone, rebirths gone...
But
You and I are not...
Because...
It's been more than loved "souls" ...
Believe in one another and one is understandable to one another
The holiness in two bodies and divine in two hearts
More than consecrated in our mind...
There is to be passionately devoted for such a beautiful and an emotion of love...
So...
It's associated with the birth of births our bond...
We are immortal and god's people
We are appearing in every lush "loved-pairs" in this world...
And
We have an untold "MAGIC" love story...
Let's create a wonderful new love story in another planet...
By god's grace!!!
Love you all...

OPEN LETTER TO TRUE LOVE

At a glance, you came into my thoughts and went away as an angel. I could not believe that the time has just moved into 5 years since I met and fell in love with you.

The minute when I am imagining you, I bounce to a different universe where you adore me as the genuineness in nature.

You did a magic to my heart, it tunes into your heart and create the affectionate waves to make a good time.

My love is an emotion, it shows an own ego something that every time needs and dies for you! My love is an expression; it goes on, no end in our bond! It is something that feels the feeling of freedom in faith.

You are the best feel that has ever happened to me. I can only hope you will be in my life forever just like you will forever in my heart.

There are so many colorful flowers on the earth but their shadow is black, the color of natural and pure love. To the world, you are a beauty but you are my beautiful world!

You are an art in my heart and breathe of my life. Never make "Y.O.U" into 'years of unhappy'!

Look into my eyes and feel my love. Join my walk of life, I will be your armor my lucky charm.

Yours
J. Naresh Kumar

NANO TALES

I

The story ended between two hearts
But
Where ended...
The new story began by two "souls"….
Because
The love is a secret in this universe
The two and together will make a magic

II

The pain is art in their "HEART"!!!
The love dissolved in their "BLOOD"!!!
The agony and anxiety are their "HAPPIENESS"!!!
The moment of time is "BREATHE"!!!
The inseparable "SOULS"… living "APART"!!!
Till they "MEET"!!!

III

Your life is your true story…
Write well, edit often...
But, in your life …
The love comes only once …
Make it pure and wonderful…
Truly accept it and move on…
Don't spoil and mystify it!!!

Kinshuk Gupta

A young poetry enthusiast, Kinshuk Gupta writer under the pen name of 'Vitaan' which means 'the sky'.

As his pen name, his poems and stories delve into complex and vast psychology of man.

He also writes a page 'Khwaishyen' on facebook in which he relates his grieves and insatiable desires of mind as a teenager. Adolescence is one of his most relished topic.

He loves experimenting with different genres. He is an avid reader and a nature lover.

Especially he loves to make and create new dishes in his kitchen like fusion style food.

NANO TALES

I

Whole his life, he dreamt of eating wheat-flour.

The day he ate it was his last day. He was allergic to wheat.

Desires are vague.

II

Her disease came in the way of her fasting for her husband.

Her healthy husband died that year.

She blamed herself whole her life.

III

The infant was critical. His father was doctor. The father did half- hearted treatment and infant expired.

He believed the soothsayer that the child will die in 1 year.

Kriti Singh

The sublime girl, Kriti Singh. She is always happy and one of the most smiling girl. You would never see her sitting idle. She loves writing and Dancing.

She is passionate about whatever she does and sure she will engrave her name in the wall of fame soon.

She has interest in writing. When she isn't glued to a computer screen, she spends time playing with kids, listening songs, reading books, learning new skills and volunteering activities.

She is very bright and studious student in her school and college.

She completed her MBA in HR & MARKETING.

You can reach her at KRITIDERJ@GMAIL.COM

Kriti Singh

WILL YOU

Will you be my place,
If I'm ready to be with you, like shadow and soul?

Will you be beautiful morning and sleepless night,
If I'm ready to be your friend, like forever and always?

Will you be right,
If I'm wrong, like a 3 year old kid?

Will you never leave my hand,
If staying with me is difficult, like sun and moon?

Will you make me your soulmate,
If I'm ready to stand beside you, like mirror and your
face?

Kunal Bembi

He was Born and bought up in Delhi.

Completed his graduation in hospitality and tourism from NCHMCT, IHM Gwalior affiliated to IGNOU.

Chef by qualification.

Sometimes writes, reads, a complete foodie person, into art as well, doodles a lot, currently looking out for job but previously working as an analyst into healthcare sector for international processes.

You can find him on Instagram with Mr. Doodlegasm or Kunaal Bembi on Facebook

Kunal Bembi

RUSTY POETRY

As I picked a pen to dust the rust from a piece of
paper,
I heard a scream
A scream of thoughts
Those piping hot thoughts in my mind
And I started bleeding
Bleeding through pen
Those misty cat looking eyes
Pointed straight nose
Fumed ears visible in her curls
Bee sting naked lips
Ass shaped chin
Soaked cheeks
Curly hairs hanging on her face
Stubborn expressions
Black mole on right upper lip
Her face in front of my eyes
I wrote her down through
That bleeding ink
I penned her down in
Those mystical words
She was my poetry
A rusty poetry

A BARTENDER

She is a wine
On room temperature
Pure red wine
Poured in a wine glass
He is a scotch
On the rocks
Topped with Ice
She felt nice.
Her flavor is cherished with cheese and red meat
He enjoys wine every night
She gulps down whisky in a one go.
On the count of three
She let him free
He won't let anyone touch his bottle of wine.
Those who tried are ripped
By his canine
She don't allow anyone to flirt
She who tried is swiped like a dirt.
Together they make a perfect mock-tail.

Manogna Boppudi

She is a 20-year-old jolly girl, pursuing Bachelor of Business Administration.

She belongs to Guntur, Andhra Pradesh.

She believes herself as a happy and a proud introvert.

She can be contacted on Instagram as manogna_boppudi

LOVE

Love me like the rain,
That freshen up my heart…
Love me like the breeze,
Soothing my soul…
Love me like the stars,
That twinkle every night…
Love me like the moon,
Giving me hope…
Love me like the pain,
That doesn't go in vain…
Love me like the paint,
Knowing me in depth…
Love me like the life,
That gives me a reason to live…
Love me like the love,
For no one can define it…!!!

Minarva Priyadarshini

Minarva Priyadarshini belongs to Odisha.

She has completed her masters in Chemistry presently.

She is a passionate writer, reviewer, blogger and an avid reader. She writes quotes, poems and stories basically on love genre.

She is a published writer in some Anthologies. One of her debut book (Poem collection) is going to be published very soon in her own language Odia.

Besides reading and writing she likes long drives and listening music.

You can get connected to her through:

Email- minarva29@gmail.com

Instagram- 29minarva_writers

Facebook- Minarva Priyadarsini

BLANKSPACE

I got a letter from
A heap of memories.
That was painted with colors of love though,
But had faded with the passing time.
I returned to the past again…
To that darkest world.
That was glittering with fireflies…
Covered with warmest wrapper of night.
Spreading a fragrance like first rain when touches the earth.
All were as usual at their places.
But, your absence,
Was covering my eyes and heart slowly.

INSIDE A PAGE

Ticking of clock,
Roaring of darkness.
Trees covered with sprinkling dew drops
And the moon.
Near an open armed window
With a cup of coffee…
A sip of it freshen up the mood.
Towards scary night to romantic dreams.
The flame of lamp,
Burning undisturbed like happy glittering eyes.
A pen in my hand,
Eyes filled to pour out emotions
And scribble on paper.
Scribbled again and again
Finally, a new life born with lively words
Singing melancholy song.
But, still smiling lips express the blushes
Of the fortunate birth.
Conveying its agony mixed glee to all.

NANO TALES

I

SHE: I have a dark page in my past.

While dropping emotions with a big sigh, she said…

HE: What if, I tear that page and put it into fire?

Will still that remain?

While wiping her tears…

HE: There will be some ashes having completely no identity.

II

SHE: My story ends with an agony.

By holding her hands and looking into her eyes…

HE: I will heal it with a happy beginning and your countless smile.

Will paint it with our love colors.

III

After five years of their break up…

HE: Will you still love me?

SHE: God has given me a power to hide my pain.

Nehal Maheshwari

An architecture student by choice and a writer by chance.

Nehal was born and brought up in Jaipur and lives there with her family.

With a few stories published in her name writing has been her way to connect to people and you can always get in touch with her at maheshwari.nehal245@gmail.com or on Instagram as @preciselychaos

OPEN LETTER:

From his Best Friend to a person very dear!

The one always by my side and the one who is my highlight of forever!

For a person just special...

I've seen you grow, I've seen you struggle, and I've seen the happy face and the side no one knows. I've had the drama and the angry bird mode; I've got the hugs and the harsh words. I've had it all yet it's always a new phase to be a part of.

A lot of things have changed; we've grown older, and wiser.

If I miss something, I'd say the time, we've got busier as well, but the bond, it has just got fonder, and healthier and of course stronger than ever before!

I cherish us, it's not just love, it's the respect that keeps us going, it's not just love but the friendship that's the base, and it's not just love, but everything else all at once. It's a dream, a dream that came true!

To a person very dear!

The one always by my side and the one who is my highlight of forever!

OPEN LETTER:

To a long distant friend, with love!

Though miles apart, considering we were stuck like glue since long, obviously the transition will take some time getting used to, but then as I sit and get all anxious about you not being here, I realise that what if we're miles apart, distance doesn't matter when it comes to the heart, right?

You know I'll always be there for you as I know you'll always be there for me. If you ever need me for anything, I do mean anything, know that I'll be there in a flash. When you feel homesick, have some boy trouble, even need help on assignments, you know that I'll gladly pick up the phone even if the conversation does drift into spending hours talking about our pathetic jokes and your sleeping sessions.

When I look at you, I actually am amazed by your independence, and your desire to take on the world. I know you will do great things, and I'm so proud of you. And I know things would change but the bond we share, I promise I'd never let it fade. If anything I know it will get stronger.

NANO TALES

I

"I know you better than you.

Calling and telling useless reasons, admit, is just your another **trick** to talk to me!", she said.

"I know it makes you happy, so why not?", He smirked.

II

It wasn't ever about how she felt but more about the way he made her feel, for her, him and them!

III

There were no stars in the sky that night, still a twinkle in her eyes!

They'd met for the first time after all.

Nitika Bansal

Nitika Bansal is a Senior Test Engineer, who loves to express the expression of life.

She hails from the beautiful twin capital city, Chandigarh.

She loves to dance and pen down her feelings and emotions which not only describes her day but also gives her an insight and understanding of the world and people around her.

She is a multi-lingual writer communicating well in Hindi, Punjabi and English.

Her dream as a writer is to write a love story someday.

I WISH

When you told me you wanted to hug me,
I wish I could have said please do,
When you said you wanted to kiss me,
I wish I could have said yes,
When you said you wanted to take me on a
date,
I wish I could have said let's go,
When you said be mine,
I wish I could have said mine too,
I wish I could have made your every wish true,
I wish I could have moved the earth and the
moon for you,
I wish our parallel world could someday
collide,
I wish.
I wish for you and for you to be mine…

OPEN LETTER:

Hey! It's been a long time since I have talked to you. When I last saw you were down-trodden by the comments of this society.

You were carrying the heavy burden of what and who is watching and criticizing you. You still get that feeling sometime, that gut wrenching thought when you are afraid that you have done something wrong or something that is not up-to the expectation of the one standing in front you.

You have always been the one who is a stickler for rules and I don't know why but you can't set yourself loose from that. But you know I am really proud of you because you have realized that you cannot change yourself but you can learn how to handle those situations which earlier used to undermine your self-confidence.

You have matured enough to know the intentions behind any criticism and to know when to improve form them and when to ignore.

Dear me! Dear you! it doesn't matter who the you are, if you related to it you are not alone here in this world, if you didn't I am proud of you for handling yourself so well so far.

-Niti

Om Parkash

Om Prakash is his birth name, but he uses under the name of Parkash pencia as pen name.

He belongs to city Abohar, Punjab.

Professionally he works in PNB as Head Cashier.

Writing is hobby and passion for him.

Along with writing, he takes interest in teaching literature.

He can be contacted via his email i.e.

parkashpensia@gmail.com

Om Parkash

WITHOUT YOU

Without you I wander as Antelope does into Burnt
bushes of fear
Not finding shelter of its choice
While I am Remaining encaged into unslept heart
Not breathing even once from desire
Eating sobs of aches till soul
Forsaking all colors of easiness from my mind
Adapting clime of mourning forgetting tears
Shedding tears of silence perhaps hidden from
visibility
Home of loneliness will bite my core
I am no more holding peace inside senses
An unending paralysis will hold my nerves
It's demise of my all wishes
Totally submerged into passion less sea
Faithless world is Gulping my sight
And I am Succumbing to my silent injuries
Given by my Mortal loneliness.

YOU

I read those tales where fancy lead me to you
My fantasy adores you in my craving silence
I cuddle with dreams consisting us
Hugging and clasping our favorite reminiscences
I don't retire from your even tiniest feelings
I relish eternal spring inside my thoughts
As you bring blooming of redolence
Repairing all my feeble or firm Ruins
Curing my all scars of loneliness
Coating my lazy wounds with your active love
And I am no more Dormant in my feelings
I am blessed with what I was Longing from ages
A kind heart with extra indigenous love
I am fulfilled with Satiating my desert soul
All pastures of my body are in festive season
All banks of my desires are Jam-packed with smiles
I am sailing not alone,
But in pair, well wedded with her all flaws
And committed to be eventually one till final demise.

Pooja Khurana

Pooja Khurana has done her Master's in English literature that led her to embrace the love of poetries and short stories.

More than 14 National and International anthologies and 14 years of writing career gave her a head start to follow the passion of writing.

She dedicates all her work to her beloved father who gave her the courage to follow the passion against all odds.

NANO TALES

I

Her ring finger was bleeding so was her soul when she bruised it while wrenching out her dead relation and threw it out from her heart's window to never look back.

II

I hated getting up with weird sensations, sleeping with rollercoasters of emotions and growing numbers on weighing scale. I almost died birthing you. Saw you in my arms and life smiled.

III

I am 24. First time I saw the brook, shinning sun, birds flying. Saw an elephant eating sugarcane. In excitement I moved the fingers on braille and started loving life.

Priyasi Das

She is Priyasi Das and she is from the City of Joy "Kolkata".

She is a Computer Science Engineering student of Techno India, Salt Lake.

Rather than being a student she is also an Author, Writer, Blogger, Poet & a daily feedback columnist at The Telegraph t2.

She is also an Award Winning Author of "100 Inspiring Authors of India 2018" by The Indian Awaz.

She has also been nominated for "Top 50 Influential Author's of India 2k18" by the Spirit Mania & "NE8x Online Literature Festival 2018"

Follow her at Insatgaram @priyasi_das, Twitter @das_priyasi

CAN I HAVE THE PLEDGE TO MAKE YOU FULLY MINE?

In the World of truth and lies,
I want you to be fully mine.

You taught me the eternity of being in love,
For which I am mesmerized and happy having you as
my beautiful thought.

You cared about me,
You feared about me.
You wanted me to survive in this World with all your
immortality.

My heart beats only for you
Because in this big world you are my only beautiful
truth.

I want you to share your happiness and sorrow with
me
So, that together we can reach our destiny.

With all my pride,

I want to be your bride.
Hold me up in your arms and let me have the pledge
of making you my prince charm.

YOU MEAN THE WORLD TO ME!

You are my tear, you are my fear.
You care about me because I am your dear.

You are my water, I am your ice.
You are my sugar, I am your spice.

You are my love, you are my scope.
You are my World, you are my hope.

You are my friend, you are my parent.
You are my Guardian, you are my ardent.

You are my negativity and positivity,
You are my immortal truth and you are my
generosity.

Rajeev Patel

Rajeev Patel, 27, is a CA Dropout cum Digital Marketer.

He hails from the city of Raipur, Chhattisgarh but currently residing in city of dreams - Mumbai.

Writing was never his forte, it just came by chance. Though he is an avid Book Reader and Reviewer.

He hopes to inspire many more people. He is a Travel Enthusiast. Strong follower of 'KARMA'.

He can be reached out at –

Instagram @itsrajeevpatel

Fb - Rajeev Patel & Mirakee - inkyour_thoughts,

Email Id - storytellerrajeev@gmail.com

LONG SPACES OF TIME BETWEEN US

It took me a long time to realize
That this is love,
But You're four times stubborn than me,
So trust me I'm afraid
Of how much till forever you'll take
To finally see what's between us.

NANO TALES

I

My first Nano Tale is directly from my heart, how does a female feel when she gets raped or molested. I have tried to express the feelings through my words:

"What she felt inside is unexplainable to the human eye, and it's nothing any other person can truly feel".

II

Defining "PAIN"

Pain can be beautiful,
Pain can be ugly,
It should be remembered,
But it should not rule you.

Rohit Bhatia

To know a person, you need to set an example first.

Rohit Bhatia, 23 years old soul, born in the deepness of city named Ranchi, Jharkhand.

A Contributing Writer as well as Poet of 82 Anthologies (Published), and shares his writing on India's E-magazine known as Storizen.

His debut Novella is all set to hit the stores this coming March. ♥

At present he owns a play School, and share his knowledge over his institute named: Creativity (shaping your future).

He can be contacted On Instagram: author.rohitbhatia and even via his mail id: authorohit@gmail.com.

Rohit Bhatia

ADORABLE

I crave I had 'SHE';
I wouldn't abut and felt her mien.
Under the deepness of aroma;
Over the tempo / rhymes;
I would've gone on knees, to kiss her attire.

So pulpy, so alluring;
Snug under my artillery.
I stow and clutch and swathe;
The vivacity stray and float.
Mumble that were our chants;
The sphere siesta and we walk out.
Envision 'We', to stay here;
Till we respire rearmost;
I rasp her signature;
She quaffs my cup of venom.
Both cooperatively became a teddy;
And deploy in serene in deepness of belle.

Sai Susmitha Guddanti

Susmitha is a mechanical engineer from Hyderabad origin.

She is an Aeroplane enthusiast, a path seldom chosen by women.

She learnt that she needs to express herself and fight for what she wants. That's when she started to pen down her thoughts.

She wants to be the voice of all those unheard women.

She is a versatile writer, avid reader & motivator.

She believes that, passion and faith are the keys to success.

Sai Susmitha Guddanti

WONDERLUST

I wander, all alone
in tangled thoughts
in my head.
I wonder
how could I alone
create such tangled
thoughts.
It's a mess, yet
I love to wander
and get lost in it.
There is a beauty in there,
moments that were gone,
for once and forever,
moments that never happen.
Replaying them again and again,
my heart is in perfect symphony
with my thoughts and memories.
After all its my wanderlust.
The lust for love,
the lust to get lost in unreal world.

Sakshi Saxena

Her Pen Name is "Lio_Sakshi".

She would love to tell that writing is not just her passion it's like breathing to her. o she just wants to spread endless love and happiness in this world through her words and wants to add sweetness in everyone's life even if it's a bit because it gives her inner peace and soothens her soul.

Whenever she is able to bring a smile even on one single face a day her soul feels content. She wants to be the reason for a positive change and positive impact in people's lives and that's possible only via words because they travel the fastest. She's a deep observer like she observes "BEHIND THE STAGE" things deeply.

She believes in karma as "what you will sow today is what you are going to reap tomorrow". Life is really short to get sad so keep smiling! She believes in herself the most because according to her, "it is you and only you who's gonna write your destiny via your deeds so make sure you write a history".

Sakshi Saxena

AN OPEN LETTER TO MY SOMEONE SPECIAL

His journey is a like that of a roller coaster ride. His body has so many scars that life has given him. He is the one who had grown up before his age and had seen a life closer and deeper than anyone else. He is the one who even if had an ocean of problems still will never fail to bring a smile on other's face. He is the one who keeps his family and friends at the top in his priority list and never and ever thinks of his own self. I am extremely blessed to have you. You are the greatest and the most precious blessing i have in my life. I am here to make certain vows to you-

I make a vow that i will always love you unconditionally and will stand with you as your backbone no matter what happens. I make a vow i will kiss you're each and every scar and will make them vanish by showering my immense love. I make a vow i will always look after you and my families first and then anything or anyone else. I make a vow that your dreams are mine now and i will be with you to fulfill them. I make a vow that neither i will never leave your hand nor you. I make a vow that i will protect you and my families from all the evilness and problems. I make a vow that i will be there with you in your lows and will try to bring a smile on your face and will be there to celebrate your highs. I make a vow that i will never let you sleep upset. I make a vow that how hard the things might get i will never and ever give-up on us and will make things work out. I make a vow that i will give you my best of honesty, loyalty, understanding, love, care, respect, support. I make a vow that I am yours and only yours and no one else will ever come into my life. I make a vow that only love and happiness will be there in your life. I make a vow that yours and family's happiness will be my first priority. I make a vow that i will never let you down and i will fulfill all my vows until my last breathe and even after that for ages. I make a vow that I will be there with you as your forever constant. I make a vow that it will be only "us" beyond forever and ages!!

NANO TALES

I

She - (Sneezing while resting in bed) hey babe! Can you please pass me the blanket i am feeling really cold.

He- Sure, babe (passing her a romantic smile) He came sat on the bed and took her into his arms and made her rest on his chest and whispered in her ears "what's the need of a blanket honey? When i am here to hold you in my arms and caress you with my love" and gave her a forehead kiss.

She- She felt so warm and safe in his arms that after giving him a cheek kiss she fell asleep

II

She - Hey i am solving a riddle please help me out!

He - Sure babe, what's the question?

She - What lasts even after ages?

He - Grabbed her in his arms and looked into her eyes and then slowly came near to her ears and whispered "us". She blushed and he kissed her forehead!!!

Gentlemen kisses your forehead before kissing your lips.

Sanchari Das

Hailing from the city of joy, Kolkata, Sanchari Das is a recent graduate who is currently pursuing a creative writing course to improve her writing skills and also doing a job as a part-time content writer.

She has contributed to multiple anthologies besides publishing her book of poetry, "Leisure", along with her debut novel, "Not Just a Love Story".

She aspires to become a great author someday and inspire millions of readers through her writing.

Sanchari Das

RISE FROM THE ASHES

They taught me to chase my dreams,
Fight for it, they said, however far it seems;
We won't ever push you to exile,
They said with a glamorous smile.

I believed them and aimed for the sky,
I spread my wings and soared up high;
And then they said with a huge sigh,
'Come down, you cannot fly!'

They brought me down with a threatening sound,
They chained my feet to the ground;
They clipped my wings and broke my dreams,
They shattered my hopes with their dreadful schemes.

'Curb the ocean of waves and be our slave',
They said, 'It's time we teach you how to behave!'
I crashed against the Earth and broke my heart,
With all the broken trust, I knew not how to start.

But I'm a phoenix, not born to die,
I have the strength none can defy!
So, you may hold me with all your might,
I'd still rise from the ashes and bravely fight.

Sangeeta Paik

Sangeeta Paik is a primary teacher in Odisha.

She was born and brought up in a small village Mohana in Odisha.

Apart from reading novels and reviewing.

She is an amid music lover, you should find her always occupied in her own thoughts, humming along.

Nature inspires her .she always aspires to writer by passion who started scribbling her thoughts and imaginations.

Email: sangeeta1994paik@gmail.com
Instagram: @sangeetapaik

OPEN LETTER

Dear Nanu,

Today i choose to release everything that has tried to hold me back I release the past. I release bitterness release my failure that i couldn't cope with emotions and breakdown with your sudden departure.

What i wish i could tell you now. What i wish i could give you a moment to see happiness on your face.

To the first best man in my life who watching me overhead. The 25years of memories you spent of your life being my father were moments i could never think to want to wash away.

I can still hear the echoing sounds of yours, the pain of your that you gone through while counting last breath.

In your life you gave us so much i couldn't gather myself together

 to do the same. When i want to pay you back fate play cruel game and snatch happiness.

I couldn't gather all my strength within me to speak out my heart that burred all for you.

I wish i could visit heaven if only for a day to see you.

I know we are never apart. everything i think of you, you're right here.. deep in my heart.

Your little daughter

Savitha Anand

Savitha Anand is an Educator by profession and Writer by passion.

A patriotic Indian, born and brought up in the beautiful and romantic Garden City.

She is an avid reader, blogger and a life enthusiast as well.

Passionate about books, her flair for writing was something that found its way to her heart after a tryst with destiny.

Being ambitious in a mix of Fantasy and realism her writings are of romantic genre beyond the shadow of doubts.

Success to her is daring to follow one's heart in realizing dreams so that your work resonates with your inner calling.

Savitha Anand

AU REVOIR

The conversation that started
by my 2 lettered word,
Was abruptly ended
By your 3 lettered one

The Embrace that once held me tight
Now forcibly shoved me away from you
Not giving me a clue of the agony
That would pain my life forever

I stood confused yet unshattered
Just for a single glance of you
My brain sensed the reverberation
But my core yearned for you

The unanswered questions puzzled me
But your silence spoke volumes
Undeterred and Unperturbed
Awaiting was I for your grave justification

Your love seeped into me
in various hues to play

Hoped to live in bliss
and for it to stay

Being crucified by your departure
You definitely owe me a proper closure.

Shobhit Gupta

Shobhit is an avid reader with interest in various genres of literature.

He has done MCA and Executive MBA. He is a Software Engineer by profession and running an IT start-up now.

As an IT expert, he writes technical text occasionally for magazines and online portals in English and in Hindi.

Apart from reading and writing, he loves to travel and to capture images. He loves to meet people, explore different cultures, taste variety of dishes and learn other languages.

He can be explored at www.ShobhitGupta.in or contacted at mail4shobhit@gmail.com.

You may follow him at facebook.com/gupta.shobhit and twitter.com/shobhit_gupta

OPEN LETTER TO TEACHERS

Dear Teachers,

When we were studying, we did not realize your importance. You used to be a devil for us. We used to feel that corrections meant to insult us, punishments were there as you hate us and blah.

You always kept personal problems away and maintain an ideal personality to follow. You always put an example for us. If you were not there, we would not have been able to bring our best.

Your lousy work could create a disaster in our lives. Every minute you spent in class, affected about a year of our lives.

Finally, we faced the world; the day we went for first interview or dealt with first client, the weekend we have to kill for few bucks, the moment we get scolding for our mistakes, we realized your worth but…

Ah! We have passed that era. At that moment, we could just repent.

You have been short-changed always.

Today, with whole heartedness, I want to say

"You are the creator of this world. God make Homo sapiens, you make humans. Thanks for all the corrections and punishments you gave, it was for my own good. Please keep on doing the good work."

Best wishes,

Shobhit

Shyam Sundar Agasthy

Shyam Sundar is a simple boy.

He loves to explore the world, and eager to learn new things.

Currently he is pursuing his MBA from Jamshedpur.

OPEN LETTER TO EX

Dear ex,

I had very honest feelings for you. There was a time when you were on the top of my priority list. But after few years, you proved me wrong! I was the one who always thought of fulfilling your dreams, and also found ways to overcome your weaknesses to make you strong. Why did you betray my feelings for you?

Do you remember our rock climbing? You said that you couldn't climb because of your health issues. But, I was there to help you, and also proved you wrong. We had climbed it without any trouble. I was always good to you. But, then too you chose to hurt me. You met other guys too and never told me. I didn't have any problem. I noticed that you had changed when I shifted to Bankura. I knew that you liked to make new friends but that time it was something else.

Even though we argued and fought many-a-times, we didn't wish to stay away from each other. But, the day when I saw you holding the other person's hand, my feelings for you were disrespected. But, then too I trusted you and thought that you both might be just friends. But, after our breakup you told me the reality that you like him. I was proved wrong, thank you!

Do you know what hurt me the most? I was trying to forget you and you kept reminding me of the dreams that we dreamt together and also the special moments we shared. I was hurt. But, I would thank you for this because it made me strong and taught me a great lesson. I won't repeat this mistake again. Even though your words broke my heart, it made me determined towards my career.

I hope that you will understand my feelings one day. And, that day you won't be able to reach me as I would be busy celebrating my own happiness.

Siddharth R

Siddharth R is a Business Analyst by profession and an amateur writer by passion.

Certain bad events and heartbreaks in his life brought out the writer who was inside him. Writing helped him to survive the worst phase of his life.

He is an enthusiastic badminton player and has done a couple of short films too.

NANO TALES

I

UNCONDITIONAL LOVE

They were fighting for hours sitting in a park bench

Which followed by a pin drop silence for another hour

Sitting close but both did not open their mouth now

The clouds suddenly turned black

Before the first drop of rain reached her

An umbrella covered her.

II

BIRTHDAY

They did not talk to each other for 10 months

They had huge issue between them

His birthday was so close

He was in no mood to celebrate his birthday without her

The time was 11:58 pm and it was just two minutes to go for his birthday

Slowly he heard his mobile ringing, it was her

She was the first person to wish him

What could he expect more?

III

OASIS

When she was in the desert of loneliness

I was there for her as an oasis

But when she had people around her

She left me stranded in that lonely desert

I still search for the small oasis of her love

Even though i know it doesn't exist anymore life.

Simranjeet Kaur

Simran is a teacher by Profession and a writer by heart, rather than choosing 'teacher' as a profession, the profession chose her. she is a true admirer.

Her pen started inking thoughts when she was in school and now she is working on her 'masterpiece'.

Music is her first love.

She loves to travel and explore new things and A big foodie who loves to cook as well.

OPEN LETTER TO FUTURE HUSBAND

Dear Future Husband,

Ever Since my Childhood, I was being taught about various do's and don'ts and this is just because one day I'm going to wed you.

Being a human, every girl has its dreams and so I have but we girls are often misjudged by this society on every single step.

Dear Husband let me open up my heart to you there are lots of things in this world which I am afraid to but I don't want you to be one of them. The agony is I always end up hurting myself in order not to hurt anyone for their expectations. Since one day, I have to meet your expectations too

However, Mr. Husband need not to worry I won't ever let you down as this life has made me strong enough to be your better half.

At last, I want to hit your conscience and let you remind that I am no ordinary girl and so not your proposal should be.

Love

Your Not So Ordinary Wife

Subhranshu Mishra

Subhranshu is an undergraduate student from Bhubaneswar, is a bibliophile and love reading lots of books of various interests.

Very keen on becoming a civil servant in future, his love towards social sciences has been since childhood.

A sainik school pass-out, his love for various sports and games is quite natural.

He has been an admirer of poetry and good writings. This is the first time he is applying for a competition like this, where he wants the world to know about his bit of skills in writing as well.

Subhranshu Mishra

THE MISLAID LIFE.

A groin pain that inflects my heart
From a wriggling-thumping motor
Pissing an infectious red wine
Into a poised, stagnant and vague
Lidless earthen pot, inflated with
Regretful memories and an even
More fragile present.
The mind coveted with a prepondering silence,
Erupts as a fast flowing stream
Rewinding torrents of yesterday and
unwinding desolations of tomorrow.
When the dark hovering clouds
Sway away my shadow,
The mid in a wary of subtended existence;
A numbness is felt, when the trees freeze
And breathe reposed down.
The howling heart fells prey
To the circumspections of time.
The baggages which keep on heaping,
The shoulders which keep dipping
Exposing the blisters of the soul
Reminding me the aches and strife.
Ultimately this meek little heart of mine blabbered,
"what if, a little less worries and a lot more life".

Sukhmani Gandhi

Sukhmani identifies herself as a woman of substance and change.

She has recently published her debut novel 'The Shadow of the Dark Soul' in 2015 which is a sincere dedication to Nirbhaya aka Jyoti Singh Pandey.

She was previously published in 'We are Not Alone', an anthology published in association with Mood Indigo in 2014.

Her other trysts with the written word can be seen on her blog 'www.sukhmanigandhi.wordpress.com'.

She believes the best form of expression is through quotations on the page "Ephemeral Words" and writes to bring awareness in the society.

NANO TALES

I
LITTLE SPRINGS

Warm hands enfolded,
Softly, clutching onto mine.
Eyes opening out to a world,
Anxious, for a story of thyne,
Bed sheets crumpled with glittering joy.
Inert, yet cautious - She softly sings lullaby.

II
DREAMS DEFERRED

Happenings of deferred dreams,
Create chaotic minds.
Beset and gloomy souls,
Twisted with bitter lies.
With the certainty of tides,
They hide-
In nights of terror and fear.

III

PAINTER'S DILEMMA

When the painting is done,

And you think you have won.

As, the world doesn't know yet -

If, you are the creator,

Then, I am the creation.

I will not let you beset,

In the dark night and bright light,

I will come with a story then.

Sushil Kumar Rana

Sushil Kumar Rana is a Mechanical Engineer working in a MNC.

He belongs to Balangir district, Odisha.

Apart from writing he loved Indian music, world's Cinema in any language and a traveler.

He is a published author of few anthologies and his Debut Novel "You are the best thing that happened to me" is popular among readers.

His Novel is nominated for three awards and recently won "The 100 inspiring authors award" by The Indian Awaz.

You can connect him through:

Facebook/coolsushil123

Instagram/author Sushil

Website: www.sushilrana.com

NANO TALES

I

You are never a loser,

It's your thoughts that

Eventually make you one of them,

So change it and believe in yourself.

You are always a winner, just give time to people, to realize it.

II

Every storms do not come for destruction of your path,

Few comes to show you better way of life

With a new beginning, isn't it?

III

"Memories are like gems, it's shinning day by day."

Holding the coffee mug at Rahim's cafe shop, Rudra remembered that unknown girl's word echoes in his ears. She is the reason for his success in the literature world.

Tanu Sharma

Tanu, a graduate belongs to the city beautiful. Profession is IT though heart and passion belongs to writing.

Long walks and sitting by lakeside soothes her soul.

Found her skill for writing through friends whom she showed her poems. Inspired by their feedback she pens down her feelings in her poems and stories.

She believes that writing helps her to see the silver lining of every situation in her life. Her creations could be read on her Facebook page "Dil Se"

Facebook Link: https://www.facebook.com/Dil-Se-438358759655083/

5 MINUTES CALL

Our love is smitten
As distance is tall
Waiting for your
5 minute call…

We just greet each other
Suddenly can hear the beep
Waiting for all day long
And call disconnects in leap
I want to talk to you
Like walking in mall
Waiting for your
5 minute call…

There is a lot to say
Heart silently pray
Words seems useless
Feelings not able to find the way
I love you seems so tiny
In the feelings of all
Waiting for your
5 minute call…

I am under sky
You in Water
I wish this separation time
Run so faster
Soon the day will come
When we will share the common shawl
Waiting for your
5 minute call ☺

Tanya Arora

 Tanya Arora, scribbling writer from science stream. She was born in Cuttack, Odisha.

She become a best story for their life.

She believes human thoughts, since her childhood days.

She loves learning by walking on her mother's foot print. She is also one of her father's princess and teachers pet.

Interpreting and expressing was her childhood art by narrating poems to dramatization. Her works can be seen in Contrivance of Sentiments and Foian's September Edition. The aim behind her writing is to express her love without revealing and prove that every no has a yes and to spread HAPPINESS and to say what she had never said.

OPEN LETTER TO PAST

Dear Past,

Why you went away leaving us with just memories, why you left us today with nothing, I start with a happy smile that I had you in life, you came to me like stars which shined in my dark, I don't call you bad but it's just that why we can't live you once more days goes on and see we moved on can't we meet once again , give me ideas to make a time machine to meet you once more, do you know you were the one where I had those happiness which is needed , days went on and you kept my happiness with you please return if possible , that's right I smiled yesterday with one who holded my hand to walk around and dear Past you made me run to the paths untrodden and stopped them to walk away, you kept them and pushed me away, please return I want them, I want the smiles which were mine , I called a fights like love of mine, can you speak the promises which were made, can you remind them again , I search them but never get them, you say haven't that what we were to what we became, but all above that thank you that you were to weave my memories with yourself to turn back, just their a request please return if possible , I am still holding back with memories , there's everything safe and sound made to gather and surround again to become once again

Please past I request you to be in mind always, everything good or bad that's mine.

Yours Present

Tejaswi Vajinepalli

Tejaswi Vajinepalli is a final year Mechanical Engineering student from Guntur.

He is a passionate writer and an avid reader. His works got published in different anthologies.

He is a professional and experienced content writer. He has an exposure of working with different organizations like MAD, AIESEC and YEF.

He is a part of Entrepreneurship Club at College and an active participant of curricular activities.

He is an orator and a motivational speaker. He is interested in the domains of psychology and people analysis which is his favorite pass time.

You can write to him on vajinepallitejaswi@gmail.com or connect through social media.

Facebook : https://www.facebook.com/TejaswiVajinepalli

OPEN LETTER

Since my Childhood, I have had everything that I ever wished for in terms of materialistic possessions. Be it toys, food, accessories, gadgets, anything and everything.

You name it I have it but still there was this emptiness and a feeling of numbness that is spreading its wings and increasing its network all over my mind and heart.

I tried hard to figure out what that is and why is it bothering me letting me down, bringing me down, killing my productivity and making me passive. I tried and tried to figure it out but was not able to until one day it suddenly struck. The only thing that I was missing all over my entire life is the sense and feel of belongingness.

After figuring it out, I was trying to make it more clear and the main problem I faced is solace, being a single child and brought up in a completely comfy and cozy environment with no friends at neighborhood, friends of college would stay from start to end of college. Then I was the only person who was there in my life till today except for my parents.

It is hard to sustain a life without any friends in solace which is equivalent to living in exile though you are with people.

Titirsha Bhattacharya

Titirsha Bhattacharya hails from Kolkata, West Bengal.

She has recently completed her graduation with psychology major.

She loves to read in her leisure and enjoys writing.

She writes poems to express her feelings and communicate.

She would like to continue her writing in future and make a mark in the literary world.

THE JOURNEY

Don't shed a tear, there's nothing to fear.
Love seems crazy, oh trust me it's rosy
Once you go through the thorns and tears.
Once you go through the pain,
It's love that all remains.
Trust me dear... Don't have any fear.
I'll be there when you cross the road
In the destination I'll be your host.
Just don't leave the war oh my soldier,
I'll be battling through the smear.
And in the end when it's all over,
Wrap me in your arms and let the love cover.
Look me into eyes and tell me we won,
Ask me to be yours… tell me I'm a part of your soul.
I'll smile and say,
I have been always yours,
I am the part of your soul and,
Darling I'll be there for you once and forever.

Utkarsh Sinha

Utkarsh (pen name utkarshunique) is a Civil Engineer who is currently pursuing his MBA from Symbiosis International University, Pune.

He loves writing inspirational quotes and believes in keeping words simple so that everyone can connect with the words.

He is a firm believer of Power of Positivity.

He loves cooking, writing, helping out people and teaching.

He started his writing journey from 2016 and is actively involved on various writing apps such as Mirakee, Yourquote.

He loves inspiring people and making them believe that "Yes, they can"

You can get in touch with him at: utkarshsnh09@gmail.com

NANO TALES

I

Life becomes more awesome when you become biggest admirer of yourself.

II

Writing is a beautiful thing.

You know why?

Because:

W – Writing

H – Heals

Y – You

III

I tried,

I learnt,

I smiled,

That's life.

Vanika Saberwal

Vanika Saberwal is a passion oriented writer with her settled profession in Marketing.

She is also an aspiring Life coach and has been pursuing her passion for writing for some years now.

With a charming and colorful personality, she loves exploring everything and believes in positive & healthy living.

Instagram Id: @iamvanika

MAN I EVER KNEW

I knew a man
Who I don't know anymore,
I knew who he was,
Which he is no more.
I loved the man I knew,
And loving the man I don't know anymore

I could see the one
I wished, never knew
But love is unconditional
It could not see the irrational
But loving the man I don't know anymore

Hopeless hopes for better change,
When could hear "never want to change"
He is no more the man I loved
He is the man she made
But loving the man I don't know anymore

I fear to touch the shore of the end
I fear my soul to rend
My eyes wait to see the miracle
And love the man I know forever.

Zaid Khan

Zaid Khan is a teenager with profound interest in all forms of literature and his special inclination is towards poetry.

Imaginative narration of scenic images filled with intense emotions is the special feature of his poems. Contributing Author of 4 books.

His motive is to work for social equality and peace by becoming one of the best voice of unheard social sections.

He thoroughly believes in values of humanity and peaceful coexistence.

He loves reading and many great classic poets have a deep influence on him and his own poetic style.

His favorites are Gulzar Sahab and Sir Rabindranath Tagore.

BENEATH MY GRAVE

My elegant eyelids closed with
An oceanic agony of my heart,
Along the shards of life which
Sets my sleepless soul apart.
Agony of my love leaves
A crimson mark of her kiss,
On the canvas of soul which
Is thirsty for the beauty's bliss.
Beneath this land of mistrust and
Over the skies of her eyes,
I'm graving beneath my grave of
Eager emotions on the rise.
Dreaming desires of my mind
Still hold a pinch of love,
Settled in the bottom of
My memorable mystic dove.

Darkness of my grave reminds
Me about the depth of,
Heaven in her smile and
Hell in her dreams.

Our More Books

www.ingramcontent.com/pod-product-compliance
Lightning Source LLC
Chambersburg PA
CBHW020249150626
46552CB00020B/726